SHADE

STONE ROBBERS

Finally Rico could bear it no longer. He jumped to his feet.

'And where are you going?' asked Uncle Sol.

'To find Delfina,' Rico lied. The mask host cheered him on. Police or no police. He was going to kill Enzo.

SHADES

STONE ROBBERS

Tish Farrell

Evans

Published by Evans Brothers Limited
2A Portman Mansions
Chiltern St
London W1U 6NR

First published in 2009

British Library Cataloguing in Publication Data
Farrell, Tish
    Stone robbers. - (Shades)
    1. Young adult fiction
    I. Title
    823.9'2[J]

ISBN-13: 9780237538088

Editor: Julia Moffatt
Designer: Rob Walster

Contents

Chapter One
Old Enemy

YEE-OW! Rico slammed into the shaman outside San Pedro church. The prayer-man's censor reeled on its chain, whisking hot ash on Rico's hand. Rico ploughed on. No time to suck singed flesh. Or say sorry to the shaman. Delfina was alone at her market stall, and Enzo Lopez was heading her way.

Rico skidded down the stone steps not made for running. Before the Spanish built their church on top, the steep stairway had led up the side of a Mayan temple-pyramid; not that Rico cared for that old stuff. Dodging the flower seller's lily buckets, he leapt the last five steps, plunging into the busy square where firecrackers snapped, bus horns blared, and minstrels drummed and fluted for the crowds.

San Pedro's Sunday market was always like this. Pandemonium. The little highland town buzzed with foreign tourists who drove up in busloads from Guatemala City to buy crafts and visit the Mayan ruins just outside town. Mayan farmers and weavers like Delfina trailed down the mule tracks from their hilltop hamlets in the hope of selling their produce to the rich city visitors. The market was their only chance to make some money.

Rico snaked through the vegetable traders towards Delfina's stall. Ahead, through the crowd he saw his sister's ponytail whip out furiously, glimpsed the back of Enzo's shiny city suit. *Crunching jaguars.* Enzo had beaten him to it, and now a group of chattering tourists was blocking his way. Rico cursed through clenched teeth. If it hadn't been for Gran he could have waylaid Enzo sooner. If it hadn't been for his mother's words clanging in his head like a gong, making him dither.

'Rico. Don't let Gran out of your sight. You know how she gets lost.'

He did know. That's why he'd stayed like a fool at the church door. Gran was inside making offerings to the old gods now that the bishop let the Maya share the Catholic church. But you wouldn't catch Rico in there, not if he could help it. The incense and the flickering candles made his head swim. So he'd watched for Gran at the door, until he'd grown bored and turned to look at the market instead.

That's when he'd spotted Enzo. The twister had just stepped off the city bus with some tourists. He was swaggering by with two village girls, and the idiots were giving him admiring looks. It made Rico want to spit. Trust the guy to turn up when he was stuck minding Gran. She could be hours yet.

Rico felt like a chained dog. He knew Enzo would head for Delfina's stall. Knew that he'd come to cheat them a second time.

Then blood came pounding in his ears, drowning out his mother's words. His brain flashed red and suddenly he was running. He had a score to settle with Mr Enzo Lopez.

Chapter Two
Fight and Flight

As Rico edged towards their market stall, thoughts of Enzo burst like shellfire.

Enzo leaving their village and his parting shot at Rico, 'Going to the city. Gonna get rich, not like you no-hope peasants.'

Enzo coming back on a visit three months later looking like some big-shot gringo.

Enzo waving the quetzal bills under

Delfina's nose, knowing how much they needed money.

Enzo buying Delfina's handmade Mayan blouses for peanuts so he could make a fat profit selling them in the city.

Enzo sneering at Rico's native breeches that had once been his father's. The father who had *disappeared* in the civil war when Rico was small.

Enzo calling Rico, 'Dumb Indian!' then ducking away as Rico swung at him. Enzo treating Rico like a worm even though he was only two years older – barely seventeen.

Fury surged through Rico's veins. He couldn't swan off to the city like Enzo. He had to dig the family fields, chop firewood, be the man of the house. He had to.

Suddenly there were raised voices. As Rico broke through the crowd he heard Delfina shout, 'No way. Not at that price.'

She was hugging the blue and purple blouses hard to her chest and Rico flushed with pride. She might be only twelve, but she had a rare gift for weaving. It bought the medicine for their mother's bad chest, the coffee, sugar, and other things they couldn't grow in the village.

Rico fixed on Enzo's city suit and charged. 'Cheating us again, twister?' He struck the tall boy hard in the back, shoving him into a trader's chicken cages. The squawking birds burst free. Shoppers shrieked. Feathers flew. And suddenly Delfina was sweeping her wares into her gathered skirts.

'Police!' she hissed, diving under the plastic sheet behind the stall.

Rico spun round. Blue uniforms running down the alley. He snarled at Enzo, 'Get you next time, twister.' Then he ducked after Delfina and fled.

13

Chapter Three
House of Masks

They'd not gone far when Delfina glanced back. 'Where's Gran?'

Rico nodded at the church. 'I'll go.'

But Delfina pushed her blouses into his arms. 'No. If Enzo complains to the police, they'll be looking for you, not me.'

'That crook won't talk. He—'

Delfina's dark eyes flashed.

'Rico, do something right. Wait for us at Uncle Sol's.'

Then she was gone – a streak of blue skirts and jet-black hair.

Rico blinked. So what was eating her?

He dodged across the town square, watching for police, watching for Enzo. His fists were itching for a second shot, except now his arms were full of blouses. He remembered Delfina's fierce look and took the next side street.

'Later,' he muttered. 'Later.'

Uncle Sol lived on Via Cruz, in a whitewashed house. There he made his famous brightly-painted masks that locals bought for religious festivals, and tourists for souvenirs.

Uncle Sol welcomed Rico into his workshop with smiling eyes. He poured out cups of steaming coffee from the hearth

and roared with laughter when Rico told
him about Enzo. Around the walls a
hundred rainbow masks laughed too –
toothy jaguars, big-billed toucans, horned
devils, leering clowns. But when Sol heard
that Rico had abandoned Granny Ana he
said quietly, 'You should always do as your
mother asks.'

Rico frowned. He knew. If it hadn't been
for Enzo...

Now the wooden masks grinned evilly,
white fangs flashing, blank eyes boring into
his heart where anger boiled – a volcano
waiting to blow. He turned away, but
Uncle Sol saw.

'Ha, Rico-lad. Don't like my masks?'

Rico squirmed. 'It's not that. I—'

'I know,' said Uncle Sol. 'You don't like
the old ways.' He smiled sadly and took
down a jaguar mask.

'Shame,' he said, stroking the glinting fangs. 'Masks are powerful things. A man who wears this might be wise and fierce as a jaguar.' Sol glanced at Rico and then he said, 'Your father was a wise, brave man, Rico. Always remember that.'

Rico turned away. He didn't want to know. Sol replaced the mask and went back to his bench. Rico prowled the workshop, brooding and waiting.

Noon came and went but there was no sign of Delfina and Gran. Rico picked at the tortilla and beans that Auntie Marta made when she came in from market. His aunt had brought bad news.

'That Enzo's saying you and Delfina stole his money. The devil.'

Finally Rico could bear it no longer. He jumped to his feet.

'Where are you going?' asked Uncle Sol.

'To find Delfina,' Rico lied. The mask host cheered him on. Police or no police. He was going to kill Enzo.

Chapter Four
More Bad Memories

As Rico dashed down Via Cruz a dark shape jumped at him from a doorway.

'Y-you?' he choked.

'Didn't I say wait at Uncle's?'

Rico gaped at his sister's angry face, then at Granny Ana perched on a doorstep. Gran had a strange look in her eyes. Rico's blood lust died. 'What happened?'

'Granny got lost, that's what. She went searching the cemetery for Papa's grave. Then someone took her to the market café. I've been running all over town. And Enzo's spreading lies…'

She grabbed Rico's arm. 'But something weird's happened to Granny.'

'She sick?'

'No. She says she's had visions. Keeps saying the name Juan over and over.'

'She means Papa?'

'Yes. I think so. She says he's in the underworld. In a pit of darkness. That there'll be a big battle. And Yum Kaax* the Corn God will free him and bring new life.'

Rico glowered. Rotten mumbo-jumbo. Their father was dead and gone and never coming back. No wonder the city folk despised the Maya. But he leant down to take Granny Ana's arm.

*pronounced Yoom Kosh

'Come on, Granny. Auntie Marta will give you some hot coffee.'

Granny smiled up. 'My boy. My Juan. Looked for you everywhere.'

'It's Rico, Granny. Your grandson.'

Granny Ana went on smiling. 'Oh I know that,' she said, suddenly standing up.

But at Uncle Sol's Granny again called Rico by his father's name. Uncle Sol winked at Rico.

'You're the spitting image, that's why,' he whispered. For a second Rico felt proud. Then the anger boiled up. Where was his father when they needed him? Killed by the army twelve years ago. Killed for campaigning to keep Mayan customs. Dead because of the old ways. Dead in a useless war.

'Better go,' Rico said. It was a two hour walk to their village and Granny Ana was already knotting her shawls to leave.

Delfina scowled, then hissed at Rico. 'But I've only earned enough for half Mama's medicine.'

'Then that's what we'll buy.' Rico looked away. He couldn't bring himself to ask Uncle Sol for the extra money. He'd find some other way.

But as they left, Uncle Sol gave Rico a package.

'You might need this one day.'

Rico saw the space on the wall where the jaguar mask had been, and his heart sank. He mumbled the thanks that he did not feel. But as soon as he was outside he had a brainwave. Why not sell the mask? Right now. In the market. He'd not let Enzo's lies stop him, would he?

Chapter Five
At the Ruined City

The long track up from San Pedro to their home village was dismal. Fog hung like shrouds in the pines, and below, volcanoes simmered. As they went Gran told tales from the *Popol Vuh*, the Mayas' sacred book, which only added to Rico's bad mood. He muttered at Delfina, 'How come she remembers all that old stuff, but not my name?'

'Because she's old, idiot.'

'And what's biting you, little sister?'

'YOU! You wrecked a whole day's trading. Now people'll think I'm a thief and San Pedro's the only place I can sell my work to the tourists. How will we buy Mama's medicine if I can't go there?'

Rico snapped back.

'It was Enzo. Not me. I stopped him cheating you.'

'I didn't need your help.'

Rico's chest filled with rocks. Words fused like lava on his tongue. He couldn't admit she was right, not with the mask still in his pack, not when his nerve had failed and they still needed money for Mother's medicine.

They trudged on up the mule tracks while Gran droned on about Crunching Jaguar and the fourfold moulding of the world, and Rico seethed, 'The world is rotten. Let it blow to hell.'

24

By the time he saw the dark thatched roofs hung with smoke, and the dreary bean and maize plots, he wanted to scream. He heard their dog, Pisto's greeting bark, their mother's hacking cough inside the house. He couldn't face her now. He turned to the outhouse, threw down the mask and grabbed his axe.

'Chopping wood!' he yelled. Wood for the cooking hearth whose smoke only made his mother's coughing worse. He never could do right, could he?

The sun broke through the mist as Rico strode out, but he did not notice. Fury swept him out of the village, along the trail, past the far skyline glint of Guatemala City way off in the lowlands, on into ancient oak woods.

He chopped and chopped at dead branches, but still the anger drove him.

He pushed further into the darkening trees, swinging the axe like a war club.

It was sunset when he reached the Mayan ruins. Few outside Rico's village knew the ancient town was there. Granny Ana sometimes came to give thanks to the gods. The local shamans too. But Rico hadn't been here for years. So what had brought him now? He gazed with sudden awe at the crumbling temple pyramid, the broken city walls. The old stones loomed grey and silent through tall trees where monkeys chattered. They told of times when his people had ruled the whole of Guatemala and beyond; when they had lived in great cities not dirt-poor hamlets.

He shivered, pulling his felt coat closer. Something was wrong.

Then he saw that he wasn't the only visitor. Fresh tyre tracks cut across the ancient plaza, then looped back and headed off west, towards the mountain road. Rico's mouth went dry. No one in the village owned a truck. They were way too poor. The undergrowth had been cleared too, and the stone Jaguar God that he and Delfina used to play on years ago smashed in pieces. It looked as if someone had tried to prise it from the wall.

Someone, but who? Rico's spine tingled with fear. Hadn't Uncle Sol told them about the stone robbers, city gangsters who had looted the old Mayan ruins outside San Pedro? His uncle said they were dangerous men who sold the old carvings to rich foreign art dealers for high prices.

And now they'd been here?

Rico ran towards the pyramid to check for more signs of damage. He didn't see the trench until it was too late. It gaped like a hungry mouth and in he fell. Into blackness. Into the earth. Just like Granny Ana's vision.

'It's coming true,' he gasped.

And not for his father, but for Rico.

Chapter Six
Underworld

One thought wormed through Rico's brain:
If I'm in the earth I must be dead. Then his
eyes flicked open and he groaned. All was
blackness that smelled of dead things. His
head was throbbing too. He must have banged
it when he fell. High above, the trench rim
now framed a starry sky. Rico shuddered. Had
he fallen into some long-lost tomb?

He felt around nervously, waves of fear rising in his chest. Some brushwood seemed to have broken his fall, but when he moved, it creaked eerily and he scrambled to his feet. Was it wood or human bones?

'Got to get OUT!' he screamed.

Out… out… out… the tomb screamed back.

Rico whirled round in panic. Ghosts; tarantulas; snakes; scorpions – anything could get him down here. Everywhere he turned the place seemed littered with rocks. It was hard to keep his footing. Then his sandal caught in the rubble, sending him sprawling headfirst. He gasped as his grazed palms stung like fire.

'Gods save me,' he sobbed. 'I'm going to die in here.'

For ages he lay where he'd fallen, too scared to move. Fear gripped him like a jaguar's jaws and he remembered the mask that was supposed to make him brave.

'You coward,' it taunted him. 'You worm.'

Fury surged once more through the fear. That stupid old stuff. Would he never be rid of it?

Gritting his teeth, he edged back under the trench.

'Where the devil's my axe?' he breathed. 'Got to find it. Can't let the ghosts and snakes finish me.'

Chapter Seven
Unexpected Visitors

As Rico's hand touched cold iron the idea came. He pictured the ruined city above.

'A pyramid. That's how I'll get out.'

He set to blindly, using the axe to dislodge stones that lay all around him, clanging the blade to scare off tarantulas and scorpions, dragging the stones under the hole, and carefully piling them up.

Escape was a long way up, but he had to try.

Then his fingers found a carved stone and tingled with shock. Tracing the outlines in the darkness triggered a memory that he'd locked away. Papa was carrying a tiny Rico on his shoulders, showing him the ruins.

'Our ancestors made all this,' Papa was saying, one arm thrown wide, the other gripping Rico's foot like a vice. 'Engineers, builders, artists. *Our* people, Rico. Family. Never forget. The living and the dead are all one big family.'

Rico sighed. One of the rocks in his chest dissolved. One less burden. Now he saw what his father meant. It made the dark seem a bit less scary.

For hours he laboured, the job growing harder as his rock pile grew higher. But as the sky started to lighten he could see that his pyramid still wasn't tall enough. His back ached and hands bled. He clambered back into the chamber.

Now, as it emerged from night, he could see the place was huge. Was it really a tomb? He glanced round nervously for skeletons, but all he could see were large stone blocks that he couldn't shift. Perhaps he could smash them smaller with his axe. As he gathered his strength for a mighty blow, something crashed through the forest undergrowth above.

Rico froze. Had the stone robbers returned? His heart thumped: fear then fury. Crooks stealing things from his people's city. He swung the axe higher. Whoever they were, he'd give them a fright.

Chapter Eight
Yum Kaax

Rico gasped. He recognised that yelp.
He scrambled back up the pyramid just
as Pisto's tawny snout peered down.

'Pisto. Good boy!'

Soon there was another face. Delfina's.
She grinned and threw down a banana-leaf
parcel.

'Hello, big brother. Want some breakfast?'

Rico tried to hide his relief.

'What kept you?' he said, ripping open the leaf and pulling out the warm tortillas. He was starving.

'We thought you'd stayed at Miguel's house. Like you always do when you're cross.' Delfina dropped to her knees.

'Heavens, Rico, what is this place?'

'Careful, sis. Don't want you flattening me.'

'Thanks.' Delfina went on craning forward. 'It's amazing,' she breathed. 'Granny said you were in a dark hole. She woke us in the middle of the night and kept talking about the visions. In the end Mama sent me to Miguel's and that's when we found out you weren't there. Everyone's out looking for you, but I knew Pisto would find you first.'

Against all odds Rico began to smile.

'You didn't bring a ladder then?'

'No. The others have a rope. Granny said to. Looks like we'll have to believe her visions now.'

Rico pulled a face. 'Thought she said something about stupid old gods and a big battle?'

'Um, well. P'raps she was wrong about that bit. I'll get the others.'

Suddenly Rico remembered the stone robbers. He needed to warn her.

'Hey, Delfina,' he called up. But she was gone.

Rico perched on his rockpile and finished the tortillas while Pisto watched.

'Those gangsters won't come in broad daylight, will they, boy?'

Pisto grunted, resting his chin on his paws. Above, the forest rang with birdcall and monkey chatter and the morning sun slid past his nose into the great underground room.

Rico's eyes prickled with tiredness. At first he thought he was dreaming. Red-gold splashes danced across his gaze. He climbed back into the chamber for a closer look.

'Crunching jaguars, Pisto!'

Rico stumbled back in horror. For out of the far chamber wall rose the mighty figure of Yum Kaax. There he was, the great Corn God, creator of all, shimmering to life before Rico's eyes.

'NO!' he yelled. 'NO. I don't believe in you!'

Chapter Nine
Discovery

'Yum Kaax has returned.'

The news spread like a grassfire through the highland villages. People flocked to the ancient city bringing flowers, incense and candles. They used woven slings to lower Granny Ana and Rico's mother into the ground, and shinned down ropes and ladders. Soon the chamber was filled with wide-eyed, silent villagers. By now they had all heard of Rico's mishap and Granny Ana's vision, and were waiting to hear more.

Granny was lighting candles and placing them beneath the magnificent wall painting that covered the wall. Rico watched her in confusion. The Corn God had looked so real earlier, as if he were rising out of the wall. Even now, when Rico knew it was only a painting, he could swear that Yum Kaax was watching him.

'Why me?' he wanted to yell.

Then Granny Ana began to speak with surprising authority.

'In this picture,' she said, 'we see the Corn God returning from the world of the dead to bring us new life. He is bringing us new hope and prosperity. We Maya suffered much in the war. Now we will have a better life.'

Excitement rippled through the listeners. Many turned to shake Rico's hand. Some women even hugged him. His mother wept joyful tears. And when Delfina glanced his way there was a new look on her face: was it respect?

Rico squirmed and shrugged at Miguel. He didn't want to know about this old stuff. He didn't want everyone's thanks. All he wanted was the Corn God's gaze to stop boring into his head.

Suddenly he heard his own voice bouncing off the chamber walls.

'The stone robbers,' he cried. 'They'll be back for the painting.'

Everyone began to talk at once.

'But how did the thieves find our old city—?'

'These city gangsters stop at nothing—'

'They have guns—'

'The San Pedro mayor should send police to guard it.'

The villagers' eyes were now wide with worry.

'No,' Rico yelled. 'Yum Kaax is ours. *We* must guard him.'

Chapter Ten
Heart of the Jaguar

Later that day Rico was brooding in the outhouse at home when Delfina and Miguel came looking for him. Delfina's eyes flashed.

'Rico, no one wants to help us guard Yum Kaax. The elders are going to San Pedro to report everything to the mayor and ask him to send a police guard.'

'But Rico,' Miguel said. 'The mayor won't care. He's Ladino. He thinks old Mayan things are rubbish. He—' Miguel broke off.

He caught Rico's eye, but Rico said nothing.

Delfina tossed her head crossly.

'It's no good waiting for the mayor to send guards. We need to do something now. The stone robbers'll soon hear that we've found the painting. They could come back any time. I think the grown-ups are just plain scared.'

Miguel nodded.

'My dad says it's because they still remember the war. They just want to keep clear of trouble.'

Delfina frowned.

'Surely we can get someone to help us.'

'There's my little brothers,' Miguel said,

'I'll send them along the track to watch the mountain road. They'll spot a truck coming hours before it can reach the ruins. That'll give us some warning.' He looked expectantly at Rico.

Rico still said nothing. His thoughts tossed and turned. Why did he care so much about the wall painting?

'Because it's ours,' said a voice that sounded like Papa's.

'Because we mustn't let it be broken up and stolen by strangers to sell to other strangers,' his own voice added.

At last he said, 'Sometimes you do have to fight for something. I never knew that till now. I hated Papa for fighting for Mayan rights and getting killed. But now—'

He unwrapped Uncle Sol's jaguar mask and held it to his face. Miguel whistled in admiration. Rico struggled for the right words.

'This helped me when I was underground,' he said. His voice sounded strange behind the mask. 'Just the thought of it. I – I can't explain…' He saw Delfina's sudden smile, like sun through a highland storm.

'Wear the mask, Rico,' she cried.

'Yeah, Rico,' cried Miguel. 'Keep it on. When the other kids see it, they'll come and help us. We'll fight like devils if we have to. Who needs grown-ups?'

'Let's go then,' said Rico, jumping to his feet. 'We've a trap to set.'

Chapter Eleven
Deadfall

It was twilight the next night when Miguel came running to the ruins.

'Truck,' he gasped. 'No lights – coming up the mountain road.'

Thirty Yum Kaax guardians grabbed hoes, ropes and scythes and shot into the undergrowth. Rico's heart thumped. Had he done the right thing stirring up the village kids? Some were only little. He'd never made a speech before, but when he'd put on the jaguar mask, the words had poured out as if someone were feeding him the lines:

'Will you let crooks steal our Corn God? Will you let them take something that could make all our lives better? Won't tourists pay to see this wonder? Won't they call at our villages and buy our produce? We won't need to go to the city to find work. The city will come to us...'

Crouched in the shadows of the temple pyramid Rico wondered if he'd spoken the truth. Then it was too late to think. Truck wheels slewed along the forest track. In an eye's blink the truck was there. The headlights flicked on, raking the forest. Rico gasped. Surely they'd see?

'No one move,' he hissed.

The truck kept coming, closer, closer. Rico held his breath till his lungs were bursting. Would the plan work?

Suddenly the headlights dipped as if dropped down a well. Timbers cracked. Metal screeched and the truck nose-dived into the trench that they'd dug across the track. The driver revved and revved. From behind the pyramid Rico heard Delfina cheer. It was she who had made the clever weave of branches and grass to disguise their trap.

'Now!' Rico yelled.

Out of the shadows leapt horned devils, fanged monsters, grinning conquistadores, and at their head, a snarling jaguar. The masked guardians charged the upended truck, smashed in windows with hoes, dragged out the terrified occupants. A gun clattered across the bonnet.

'Quick. Tie 'em up,' cried Miguel.

Next there was movement in the trees. Rico turned in alarm. Not more stone robbers? But out of the dark rushed a crowd of villagers, and on their heels, Granny Ana with a lantern.

She beamed at Rico.

'I knew you would fight to save Yum Kaax. So like your father.'

But when she turned to the villagers there was anger in her voice.

'Didn't I say you were cowards to let your young ones fight alone. See how they have won already.'

A dozen fathers now rushed forwards and soon had the stone robbers tied up like a string of mules. Five men and a youth hung their heads at the jeers and insults.

'We'll march them down to San Pedro right now,' said Miguel's father.

Rico pulled off the jaguar mask, relieved for someone else to take charge. It was over.

But then light from Gran's lamp caught a familiar face.

'You!' Rico yelled, grabbing Enzo's shirtfront. 'You led these crooks to our ruins? To steal from your own people?'

Enzo's eyes flashed with hatred.

Rico balled his fist. Now at last he had Enzo Lopez exactly where he wanted him. Helpless as a trussed-up chicken.

Chapter Twelve
Fame and Fortune

The stone robbers' dramatic capture was talked of in the highlands for weeks, but it was Rico's discovery that made world-wide news.

2,000-year old Mayan mural
miraculously discovered.
Village boy finds priceless art treasure.

The first visitors to the ruins were museum officials from Guatemala City. When they said they would pay the villagers to guard the wall painting from other stone robbers, Rico was the first to volunteer. It wasn't just for wages either, much as they needed the money. There was something else.

As he patrolled the ruined city with Miguel he relived the moment of Enzo's capture, wondering if there could have been a different ending.

For just as he'd raised his fist to smash Enzo's smug face, a strange thing had happened. His hand had dropped to his side and he'd found himself saying, 'Better to be a dumb Indian than a dumb thief, eh, Enzo?'

The fury that had boiled so long inside simply fizzled out like dousing a bonfire. In fact he'd started to laugh, holding up the jaguar mask like a trophy. It might not

have made him wise and fierce as Uncle
Sol said, but he felt good. As if he'd
escaped from a deep, dark place. He did
have the mask to thank for that. And
finding Yum Kaax. And maybe, just maybe,
the old ways weren't so bad. He meant to
find out. When the archaeologists arrived
to excavate his people's city he would be
sure to ask them.

Author Note

This story is entirely fictional but it was inspired by a real and accidental discovery made by in 2001 by an American archaeologist. He was visiting some Mayan ruins in the Guatemalan forests and stumbled into a trench cut by 'stone robbers' who had been looking for ancient carvings to sell. The trench led to an underground chamber and around the walls, although mostly hidden by a layer of mud, was one of the finest Mayan murals ever found.

The setting, then, is today's Guatemala, a Central American country that was once part of the Mayan Empire. The Maya are famous for magnificent stone-built cities with pyramid temple platforms. This great civilisation developed over at least 2,500 years, but came to an end in 1530 when the Spanish conquistadors invaded and established Spanish colonial rule. Mayan land was taken for large plantation agriculture and Mayan culture and beliefs were suppressed. Until recent times the ruling class were mainly people of Spanish descent. There is also a mixed race, Spanish-Mayan population known as Ladinos.

From 1960-96 there was a civil war. Many thousands of Maya were killed or 'disappeared' by government forces. Even today many Guatemalans do not know how or where their loved ones died. Often their only crime was to claim the right to wear Mayan dress, speak their own languages and pray to their own gods.

In *Stone Robbers* the Catholic Church where Rico is waiting for his grandmother has been built on top of a Mayan temple. This was done in the past by invading Spanish in an attempt to suppress Mayan beliefs. But now the Maya are allowed to worship there again in their own way, and their shamans or day keepers have come out of hiding. The church and the town of San Pedro are loosely based on the real Mayan market town of Chichicastenango, a favourite upcountry destination for foreign tourists who go there to see the colourful markets.

Although there have been many improvements since the civil war, life for most young Maya is still very hard. Their families are too poor to send them to school so they have to work for a living as soon as they can. Many leave their villages to find work in Guatemala City as Enzo does. Some end up living on the streets and turning to crime. Others, like Rico and Delfina have to stay in their highland villages and rely on making some cash for necessities by taking their produce to the nearest market town, often a day's walk from their homes. The Maya are still second-class citizens in their own country and, sometimes, foreign tourists do not always respect the Maya or their sacred customs. For Rico, living this kind of life makes it hard for him to feel proud of himself.

Look out for these other great titles in the *Shades* series:

Animal Lab
by Malcolm Rose

Jamie hates the fact he's
gone bald. But can it be
right that the animal lab
where he works is using
monkeys to find a cure?

Mind's Eye
by Gillian Philip

Braindeads like Conor
are scary. Or that's what
Lara used to think....

Four Degrees More
by Malcolm Rose

When Leyton Curry see
his house fall into the sea,
there's nothing he can
do...
Or is there?

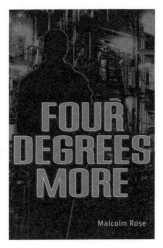

Hauntings
by Mary Chapman

Rebecca Jane opens her
birthday presents and
walks into a living
nighmare, because a
ghostly presence appears
to be taking over her
life...

Cuts Deep
by Catherine Johnson

Devon's heading for
trouble till he meets
Savannah, and starts to
change. But can he ever
put the past behind him?

Virus
by Mary Chapman

Penna's life is
controlled by a computer
programme. Until a
virus gets into the system
and the whole world is
under threat…

Man Trap
by Tish Farrell

Danny doesn't want to be a hunter, but the rains have failed and he and his father must go out poaching or his family will starve. Then Danny makes a fatal mistake…

Danger Money
by Mary Chapman

Bob Thompson is thrilled when he goes to work on the Admiral, an armed smack defending itself against German U boats. But it's not long before he really has to earn his danger money…